STORY BY
MARGIE PALATINI

PICTURES BY
GUY FRANCIS

MARY HAD A LITTLE HAM

PRESENTED BY
HYPERION BOOKS FOR CHILDREN
NEW YORK!

First Edition
1 3 5 7 9 10 8 6 4 2

Printed in Hong Kong by South China Printing Company Ltd.
Library of Congress Cataloging-in-Publication Data on file.
ISBN 0-7868-0566-8

Visit www.hyperionchildrensbooks.com

For all of my family "hams"
—M.P.

For my little piggies
Calvin, Samantha, Madeline, and Max
—G.F.

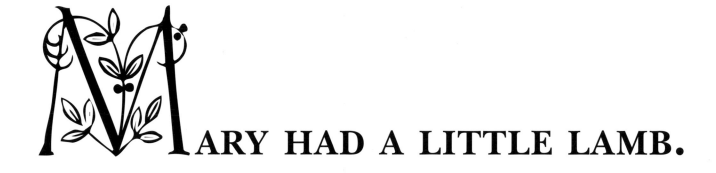

MARY HAD A LITTLE LAMB.

Wrong! That's right. Hold on to your woollies. . . . There was a boo-boo with the baa-baa. The old Goose Lady got her tails mixed up.

What Mary had—was a little *ham*. A corker of a porker! Stanley was the last in the litter of the Snoutowski brood. He was quite handsome. Very pink. And *extremely* talented.

Mary knew Stanley had that "special something" right from his very first oink.

He was not one of those little piggies that went to market. Uh-uh.

Nor was he one of those little piggies that just stayed home. Nope.

He did not pig out. Ever. In fact, he was a little piggie who rarely ate roast beef.

And Stanley, as wee as he was, certainly was no crybaby. No, no, *no*!

Stanley was an *actor*. In fact, a regular little ham.

He could make 'em laugh.

He could make 'em cry.

And, wow! Could those little pig's feet hoof it!

Stanley could do it all. He was very versatile.

Mary was Stanley's biggest fan.

"Stanley Snoutowski, you're wonderful!" she would say.

She was his best audience.

"Bravo, Stanley! Bravo!" she would applaud.

And Mary always told him she thought he was the most talented pig she had ever met.

"Stanley, you're the most talented pig I've ever met."

The two became inseparable.

Everywhere that Mary went, Stanley was sure to go. It wasn't too surprising when he followed her to school one day. Yes, he knew it was against the rules. But he wanted to make the children laugh at his new play.

They did.

"We love Stanley!" they all squealed, swooning over the little swine.

Well, Mary knew that with that kind of talent, there was no keeping Stanley down on the farm just doing summer stock. No doubt about it, the little pig was headed for the bright lights of Broadway.

The two friends promised to write and always keep in touch. Mary kissed him on the snout for good luck. "Remember, Stanley," she said, as they both waved tearful farewells, "you're leaving here a pig, but you'll be coming back a star!"

Stanley went to forty-two cattle calls that very first week in the city. There were hundreds of hams just like Stanley at those auditions, all hoping to land their first pig part in the theater.

But the directors were not interested in Stanley—or his talent.

Before he even had a chance to finish singing, he would be ushered to the exit.

"Mi mi mi—"

"Too short. NEXT!"

And, "La la la—"

"Too chubby. NEXT!"

And again, "Fa la la?"

"Lose that honker of a nose and change the name. NEXT!"

"Huh?"

"You're boring me, kid. Boar-ing!"

With little success, and after much rejection, Stanley began to doubt himself and his talent.

He wrote to Mary, *Am I really too short? Should I shed a few pounds? Could I spare a few ribs?*

He pondered his portly profile in the mirror and waited to hear from his friend.

Of course, Mary wrote back immediately. *Nonsense! Pig slop!*

Mary was right, thought Stanley. He was a fine-looking hunk of a pork. A bit stocky, perhaps, but nonetheless, handsome. Pink. Proud!

Change his snout? Never! Switch his moniker to the likes of *Hamilton* or *Bacon*? No sirree. It would be SNOUTOWSKI lit up in lights on the marquee for all to see!

Right there and then it seemed impossible. Improbable.

Then Stanley thought of Mary. She believed in him.

"I believe in me, too!" the little pig sang out. Stanley had a feeling way down deep inside that he was going to make it, no matter what. It was going to mean hard work. Lots of determination. And probably some luck, but . . . he was going to do it!

However, pig parts were few and far between. Oh, yes, Stanley did get a small part, here. He managed to get his pig's foot in the door, there. But while waiting for that big break, Stanley, like a lot of young actors, had to bring home the bacon by working as a part-time taxi driver and singing waiter.

Days passed into weeks. Weeks passed into months. Then more months.

Yes, people knew the name Stanley Snoutowski. . . . Unfortunately, the only place they knew it was at the restaurant.

"Snoutowski! Burgers and fries for table number four— and make it snappy!"

Back on the farm, Stanley was still in Mary's thoughts. She kept saving her pennies for the day when she knew she would see her little ham starring on Broadway.

And she wrote him once a week, always with an encouraging message.

Just remember, Stanley! Sing out! Sing out! You can do it!

"I can do it!" Stanley said aloud one day while driving his taxi. "I will do it!"

Then, just at that moment, who should hail his cab on the corner of Central Park South and Fifth Avenue but none other than the famous Broadway producers Hoggers and Hammerswine.

"Take us to the Forty-second Street Theater, my portly young pig," said Hoggers as he and Hammerswine climbed into Stanley's cab.

 With the meter ticking, his heart beating, and the letter from Mary by his side, Stanley got into gear, got up the gumption, and—sang out with gusto! "Right to the a-ven-ue, I'll take you to—Forty-second Street!"

 Hoggers looked at Hammerswine.

 Hammerswine looked at Hoggers.

 "He's—he's—he's *spigtacular!*" declared Hammerswine to Hoggers.

 "He's—he's—he's *snoutstanding!*" declared Hoggers to Hammerswine.

 By the time the taxi got to Times Square and Stanley had sung an overture and three choruses, the producers wanted him for their new Broadway show!

HAMADEUS

Pork Chop on a Hot Tin Plate
STANLEY SNOUTOWSKI
and PENELOPE PENN

THE PORK LOIN KING
THE BROADWAY MUSICAL

This is Maggie the Pig...

South Pigcific

HOGGERS and HAMMERSWINE'S
OINKLAHOMA!
with
Stanley Snoutowski
and
Sue E. Pigg

PIGMALION

STANLEY SNOUTOWSKI
IN
The Pig and I

BEAUTY AND THE BACON
A NEW MUSICAL

Stanley became an overnight success!

His name was up in lights. Critics raved. Everyone who was anyone was talking about Stanley Snoutowski!

He was a smash in *South Pigcific*.

Then he was box-office boffo in *The Pig and I*.

"He did it!" they cheered him in *Pigmalion*.

Stanley even won the Best Actor of the Year award, for his role in the famous play *Pork Chop on a Hot Tin Plate*.

And then, he got the piggest part of his entire career! The lead in *Hamlet*.

However, Stanley wondered if he could really cut the mustard in one of Sheepspeare's classics.

Opening night, backstage, alone in his dressing room, Stanley put on his greasepaint . . . and worried. He put on his costume . . . and worried. He waited for his cue . . . and worried.

Stanley had a bellyful of butterflies. Could he really do it? He wasn't at all sure the show could go on!

And then he read the note that Mary had sent to his dressing room: *Dear Stanley, the world is your stage. You can do it! Your Friend, Mary.*

There was a knock on his door. "You're on, Mr. Snoutowski! Break a leg!"

Stanley put the note in his pocket. He waited in the wings. The houselights dimmed. The curtain went up. He made his entrance . . . the spotlight was on him . . . the audience was breathless. . . .

"BRAVO! BRAVO! BRAVO!"

The applause was thunderous, the cheers deafening.

"What a talent! What an actor! What a pig!" roared the audience.

Stanley took a bow. He was a triumph! An absolute sensation!

And Mary was sitting in the balcony to see it all. She smiled.

Yes, she had always known that her Stanley had the talent. That
"special something." She wasn't surprised. Not one bit.

After all, she had known all along that her little pig was a born ham.

And that is no baloney.